Acting Edition

I0591756

Br'er Cotton

by Tearrance Arvelle Chisholm

FOR PRODUCTION INQUIRIES

UNITED STATES AND CANADA
info@concordtheatricals.com
1-866-979-0447

UNITED KINGDOM AND EUROPE
licensing@concordtheatricals.co.uk
020-7054-7200

Each title is subject to availability from Concord Theatricals Corp., depending upon country of performance. Please be aware that *BR'ER COTTON* may not be licensed by Concord Theatricals Corp. in your territory. Professional and amateur producers should contact the nearest Concord Theatricals Corp. office or licensing partner to verify availability.

CHARACTERS

RUFFRINO / SON – 14, male, Black
NADINE / MOTHER – early thirties, female, Black
MATTHEW / GRANDFATHER – sixties, male, Black
CAGEDBIRD99 – 14, female, White
OFFICER – mid-thirties, male, White
REDNECK_SWAG – disembodied White voice

SETTING

The cotton field. Timeless.
The kitchen/cotton field. A cotton field grows in a kitchen.
The kitchen is sinking.
Diaspora. A post-apocalyptic wasteland via video game console.

TIME

Right-right now!

AUTHOR'S NOTE

(Text within parentheses) indicates that the text is spoken to oneself.
Mostly.

Ars Poetica

(The cotton field.)

*(**MOTHER**, a new mother, cradling an infant. Timeless.)*

*(This is a lullaby. **NADINE** fills the beats [...] with music.*)*

MOTHER. Once upon a time out of mind, this land was one great big tall hill.

...

The hill reached up forever; higher and higher. Past the clouds, past the stars, past the moon, to where if you stood on your tippiest-toe on the very top branch of the tallest tree on the highest peak with your arms stretched out as far as it could go, the tip of your longest finger would be just a hair length from touching heaven.

...

Livin' in the shadow of heaven made everybody terribly happy. Leastwise that's what they told themselves. Everybody spoke the same language and was generally on the same accord. And even when there were moments of difference, the difference was so slight that capitulation left no lasting wounds. And everyone was contented to live this way.

...

---

*A license to produce *Br'er Cotton* does not include a performance license for any third-party or copyrighted music. Licensees should create an original composition or use music in the public domain. For further information, please see Music and Third-Party Materials Use Note on page iii.

MOTHER. Everyone except Br'er Cotton.

   ...

   ...

Everyone on the hill used the same word for "peculiar" and everyone agreed that Br'er Cotton was exactly that.

Because everyone grinned, and he scowled.

Because everyone whispered, and he screamed.

Because everyone sang

   ...

and he cursed.

   ...

Because everyone was glad to live in such close proximity to heaven, but seeing heaven's gate from his front porch only served to taunt Br'er Cotton.

   ...

"Why should somethin' so good, be just out of my reach?" he fumed. "Why can't I enjoy my heaven here on Earth?"

   ...

The unfairness of it all infuriated Br'er Cotton to the point where he could only spit and grind his teeth. 'Til this one day, no special day in particular, save it was the day that he finally made his decision. On this very ordinary day Br'er Cotton decided he could take it no longer. He was gonna break into heaven.

   ...

   ...

   ...

Two Birds

(Lynchburg, Virginia. The City of Seven Hills.)

(The eighth and forgotten "Cotton Hill.")

(The hill is taking back the house.)

(A cotton field grows in a kitchen.)

(The kitchen is sinking.)

*(**NADINE** enters. She's wearing a neon polo and khakis. The back of her shirt reads "Lovely Maids.")*

(She uproots the table and moves it to the other side of the room. She considers it. She uproots the chairs and moves them too. She considers all.)

*(**MATTHEW** enters. He wears an ancient bathrobe. It looks as if it is made of tree bark. He has tufts of cotton in his hair. His eyes are tightly closed. He stumbles about blindly. He crashes into the newly-placed table.)*

(He opens his eyes.)

MATTHEW. Damn it Nadine! Why is the table over here?

NADINE. I moved it.

MATTHEW. ...

(You moved it huh?)

> *(He considers this. He closes his eyes again and begins to make a mug of coffee.)*

> *(He makes a great show of how difficult this is to do blind. **NADINE** ignores him.)*

NADINE. I'm feng shui-ing.

MATTHEW. Feng shui-ing?

NADINE. Feng shui. It's the ancient Chinese art of furniture arrangin'.

MATTHEW. I know what it is.

NADINE. ...

MATTHEW. (Feng shui. Huh. Everythang we got is trash.)

> ...
>
> Say, I wonder what this pile a trash look like in this corner? How 'bout we slide this heap uh junk 'gainst that wall. I thank a lil of that debris'll really open up the space. Huh!

> *(He knocks over his cup of coffee.)*

Damn it!

> *(With his eyes still shut, he fumbles for a dish towel. He creates a bigger mess.)*

NADINE. Goddammit you ol' fool! Move! You just spreading the mess around! You and your stupid ol' man games.

> What are you trying to prove stumblin' round with your eyes pent up anyhow?

> *(**NADINE** cleans up his mess.)*

MATTHEW. I'm practicin'.

NADINE. Practicing for what?

MATTHEW. Not bein' able to see.

NADINE. You goin' blind now? You just come from the eye doctor and he ain't said nothin' 'bout you –

MATTHEW. Is he in my eyes? Can nat man see what I see? Ain't nothin' as clear or as bright as it usetuh be! Everythang dull! 'Cause...

NADINE. 'Cause what?

MATTHEW. 'Cause...I'm dyin', Nadine.

NADINE. ...

Well...you mind hurryin' it along. I gotta get to work.

MATTHEW. Thass cold-blooded.

NADINE. I ain't got time to be foolin' with you today, Matthew.

MATTHEW. Ain't nobody foolin', Nay! Woke up this mornin' and there Death was, lyin' in the bed next to me. Got up and shaved and there he was starin' right back at me in the mirror. Grinnin'. Thass how come I'm pretendin' to be blind; I'm tired uh seein' his face. I figure, with the way he stalkin' me so this likely be my last day on this here earth.

NADINE. Is that a fact?

MATTHEW. Sho. I think you oughta take the day off from work.

NADINE. Interestin'. That's the same mess you fed me yestaday. And like a fool I went ahead and stayed home – in spite of the fact you ain't name not a single tangible symptom. Then, soon as I call in, you miraculously got better. You even did ya calisthenics in the afternoon –

MATTHEW. Them calisthenics is the only thing that's keepin' this ol' ticker tickin'!

NADINE. I'm jus' sayin'. I ain't seen no more signs of your impending bucket kickin'. You was all better. Until now. Today. When I'm on my way out the do' again. If I didn't know no better, I'd say you didn't want me to work.

MATTHEW. Well –

NADINE. But that's crazy right? Seeing as how this family need all the money it can get.

MATTHEW. I got my retirement checks –

NADINE. Yeah, but you get your check on the first and by the fifth you askin' me to hold twenty dollars.

MATTHEW. Never you mind what I do with my check –

NADINE. Which is exactly why I gotta work.

MATTHEW. But do you gotta work for them?

NADINE. Who? Lovely Maids?

MATTHEW. No, not Lovely Maids – But yes, Lovely Maids!

NADINE. ...

MATTHEW. Don'tcha see?

NADINE. ...

MATTHEW. Do you gotta work for...white people?!

NADINE. I got all kinds of clients. I clean wherever they send me.

MATTHEW. That ain't the point, gal.

> ...

> Yuh great-great-great-grandmother –

NADINE. Who was a slave.

MATTHEW. – Cleaned some white man's house. Yuh great-great-grandmother cleaned some white man's house. Yuh great-grandmother cleaned some white man's house. Yuh grandmother, my mother, cleaned some white man's house. And yuh mother, God rest her soul, cleaned –

NADINE. Fine! I get it. I come from a long line of cleanin' women. What of it?

MATTHEW. This family stuck in a rut, Nadine! And it ain't just the women folk neither. I worked at the cotton mill, my daddy worked at the cotton mill, my granddaddy picked cotton, my great-great–

NADINE. Fine, Matthew. I get it. We in a rut. What do you want me to do about it?

MATTHEW. Unrut us!

NADINE. And pray tell, just how am I supposed to do that?

MATTHEW. Quit.

NADINE. I cain't quit.

MATTHEW. Why not? You went to college.

NADINE. We done been over this time and time again. I went to Lynchburg College for one semester! I got a total of four, count 'em, four college credits.

MATTHEW. That's more than I got.

NADINE. Yeah, but it ain't enough.

MATTHEW. Enough for what?

NADINE. You think I want to clean up after folks for a living? Don't you think if I had any other choice I'd be doing something else?

MATTHEW. I think you think it's easier for you to settle, than it is to actually try.

NADINE. Now you wait a goddamn minute! You don't know shit 'bout what I'm tryin' to do! So just shut your damn mouth, ya hear!

MATTHEW. Jesus!

...

I wasn't trying to get nothin' started here, Nadine. I just thank each generation oughta do a lil better than the one that come befo' it. How come you think I went to all the trouble of settin' the bar so low?

(RUFFRINO *enters. He's dressed in all black, with a black beret and dark shades. He looks rather militant. He has an overstuffed bookbag slung across his shoulder.*)

MATTHEW. Speak of the devil. It's Ruffrino. The last hope of the Witherspoon family legacy.

NADINE. ...

MATTHEW. ...

RUFFRINO. Wassup?

>	(*The kitchen sinks a few inches.*)

>	(**RUFFRINO** *stumbles.*)

Y'all feel that?

>	(*They haven't.*)

NADINE. Sit down, I'll make you some toast.

RUFFRINO. Naw, I'm good. I gotta get goin'.

NADINE. What's the rush? School don't start for another hour. You got plenty of time.

RUFFRINO. I'm going in early.

NADINE. For what?

RUFFRINO. No reason. I just gotta go.

NADINE. What are you up to?

RUFFRINO. Nothin'.

>	(**NADINE** *scrutinizes him.*)

NADINE. You only wear that beret when you feelin' especially "revolutionary." What are you plannin'?

RUFFRINO. Nothin'. Damn.

NADINE. That's it. Open your bookbag.

RUFFRINO. What? Why?

NADINE. 'Cause the last time you was dressed like this you got suspended for inciting a riot.

RUFFRINO. It wasn't a riot, they just panicked because of the sirens. Some fuck shit –

MATTHEW. Watch that mouf!

NADINE. Either way, ya principal said any more "rebellious activities" and he was gonna let the police deal with you.

RUFFRINO. Fuck the po-lice!

MATTHEW. Watch that mouf!

RUFFRINO. Can I go now?

NADINE. Not until you open that bookbag.

RUFFRINO. ...

Whatever.

(He heaves the bookbag onto the table.)

NADINE. Open it.

RUFFRINO. You open it.

(An impasse.)

MATTHEW. I'll open it.

(He opens the bookbag. He peers in hesitantly.)

It's paper. See Nay, nothing but papers and them ol' beat-up Black Panther books.

*(**NADINE** inspects the bookbag; she pulls out the papers. She holds up a sheet, it has the face of a young black man on it.)*

NADINE. Who is this?

RUFFRINO. D'wayne Chambers.

NADINE. He a friend of yours?

RUFFRINO. A friend of mine? You can't be that oblivious! Hello! Wake up! Read a damn paper sometime –

MATTHEW. Ruffrino!

NADINE. Answer me now! Who is this?

RUFFRINO. D'wayne Chambers. The latest casualty in the war the white man is waging on young black men in this country. Shot and killed by the police for no other reason than he was young and black and thus a threat to the establishment. Ring any bells?

> *(In response, NADINE digs deeper into his bookbag.)*

Don't look in that –

> *(She pulls out a bottle of lighter fluid.)*

NADINE. Lighter fluid? What is this for?

RUFFRINO. An art project.

NADINE. You don't have art class.

> *(She digs farther into the bag, a hidden compartment. She removes a small axe.)*

Explain THIS, Ruffrino!

RUFFRINO. I don't have to explain myself to you –

> *(NADINE steps closer to RUFFRINO. A warning.)*

NADINE. Answer me, or I swear 'fore God –

> *(RUFFRINO steps even closer to NADINE.)*

RUFFRINO. What?

> *(They face off.)*

MATTHEW. My daddy woulda laid me out where I stood if I'da bucked at my momma the way you doin' –

RUFFRINO. Then do something about it, old man.

MATTHEW. Don't test me boy. I can still knock you clean into –

> *(He lunges for* **RUFFRINO** *but loses his footing and stumbles.)*
>
> *(***NADINE*** *is distracted.)*
>
> *(***RUFFRINO*** *grabs his things and beelines for the door.)*
>
> *(But* **NADINE** *is quick. She intercepts him.)*

NADINE. Where you think you goin'?

RUFFRINO. Away!

NADINE. You ain't goin' nowhere until you tell me just what it is you plannin' to do!

> *(***NADINE*** *grabs* **RUFFRINO**'*s bookbag. They play tug o' war over the bag for several beats. Until* **RUFFRINO** *lets go.)*
>
> *(***NADINE*** *stumbles back and twists her ankle.)*
>
> *(She fights back tears.)*

MATTHEW. There. I hope you proud of yourself.

RUFFRINO. It wasn't my fault!

MATTHEW. And you used to be such a good kid, Ruffrino? I don't know what's got into you. It getting to where I cain't stand you.

RUFFRINO. I can't stand you either!

NADINE. You ain't gonna be happy 'til them people done thrown you out of that damn school!

RUFFRINO. Who cares. Nothing but zombies there anyway. The living dead.

NADINE. Well what you think the folks like in jail? 'Cause it's like you been throwing rocks at the prison lately. Thass where you wanna be? Jail?

RUFFRINO. You would love that wouldn't you? So you could pretend like I never happened just like my damn father –

> (**NADINE** *raises her hand to* **RUFFRINO***, but she catches herself.*)

NADINE. ENOUGH! ENOUGH! ENOUGH!

I am sick to death of the both of you.

MATTHEW. What I do?

> (**NADINE** *cleans up Ruffrino's mess.*)

NADINE. It's like nobody else in this house is capable of thinkin' about anybody other than theyself! Between you and your "deathbed." And you concealin' weapons, tryin' to start the revolution, I ain't got nothing left! You two are runnin' me ragged. I'm in tatters! I'M FRAYED! FRAYED!

RUFFRINO. You so damn dramatic.

> (*He tries to leave, but* **NADINE** *stops him.*)

NADINE. Oh no, no, no – You ain't goin' nowhere.

RUFFRINO. I gotta go to school don't I?

NADINE. I don't trust you, Ruffrino. And besides your grandfather is passin' on to the great by and by this afternoon, so here's what's gonna happen: Ruffrino you stayin' at home and lookin' after your grandfather. And Matthew you be in charge of keepin' this boy from self-destruction. Two birds!

MATTHEW. Nadine!

RUFFRINO. Nadine!

(The kitchen sinks a few more inches. **RUFFRINO** *is the only one who notices.)*

Nadine Cleans

(*Another room in another home. Or at least the suggestion of one.*)

(**NADINE** *cleans her life away.*)

NADINE. ...

(**NADINE** *cleans.*)

...

(**NADINE** *cleans.*)

...

(**NADINE** *cleans.*)

...

(**NADINE** *cleans.*)

...

(**NADINE** *cleans.*)

...

(**NADINE** *cleans.*)

...

(**NADINE** *cleans.*)

...

Everything

(The kitchen/cotton field.)

(A cart with a TV and a video game console has been rolled into the room.*)

*(**MATTHEW** and **RUFFRINO** sit at the kitchen table. **MATTHEW** is lost in a story; **RUFFRINO** is lost in the TV.)*

MATTHEW. ...So once he decided that he was gonna break into heaven he ate a spoonful of clabber, tucked in his socks, and set out on his journey...

*(He realizes **RUFFRINO** isn't paying attention.)*

Hello? Earth to Ruffrino!

RUFFRINO. ...

MATTHEW. HELLO!

RUFFRINO. What? Oh. Good story, Matthew.

MATTHEW. You wasn't even payin' attention.

RUFFRINO. ...

MATTHEW. Dadgummit! Hello!

RUFFRINO. What?!

MATTHEW. You ain't lis'nin' to me!

RUFFRINO. I'm busy.

MATTHEW. Busy wit' what?

...

---

*A license to produce *Br'er Cotton* does not include a performance license for any third-party or copyrighted recordings. Licensees should create their own.

(What is this world coming to when a ol' man cain't run off at the mouth and have somebody lissen at him?)

(**RUFFRINO** *stares at the TV.*)

Will you turn that idiot box off? I'm testifyin' over here!

RUFFRINO. Matthew! Shhhhhhh!

MATTHEW. ...And thass another thing, how come you callin' me Matthew?

RUFFRINO. ...

MATTHEW. HELLO!

RUFFRINO. What?

MATTHEW. How come you call me Matthew?

RUFFRINO. Because. It's your name.

MATTHEW. I know that! But it used to be in my day merely living longa than anotha person entitled you to a few inalienable privileges. One of which was the addressment by certain basic titles from they youngers.

RUFFRINO. Such as?

MATTHEW. Y'know...sir. Ma'am. Mister. Miss. Momma. Daddy. Granddaddy –

RUFFRINO. I am not callin' you "Granddaddy."

MATTHEW. Why not?

RUFFRINO. It sound sus.

MATTHEW. ...

RUFFRINO. "Granddaddy."

MATTHEW. Well, if you say it like that.

(**RUFFRINO** *returns to staring at the TV.*)

(*Suddenly:*)

RUFFRINO. Damn it! Nadine fucked everything up! I can't believe she took my shit!

MATTHEW. Hush all that cussin' –

RUFFRINO. Look at what's going on. Today was the day. I tweeted to all my followers that today was the day for my…art project. Now I'ma look like some wack loser. "Sorry guys, can't start the revolution today, my mommy won't let me out to play."

MATTHEW. Revolution? Huh.

RUFFRINO. Don't worry about it. It'll be televised.

MATTHEW. Huh. Jus' what was you plannin' to do anyhow?

RUFFRINO. Wake up the fuckin' zombies.

MATTHEW. I ain't gon' tell you again about that mouf! Show me some respect.

RUFFRINO. Whatever.

MATTHEW. Now, how you supposed to wake up these "zombies" as you say? With some lighter fluid and a hatchet? Wha's a few pictures of some dead boy supposed to do? Answer me that.

RUFFRINO. Make them think! Open their eyes. Show them: Black lives matter! Black kids, that look just like me, are getting shot down. Left and right! And nobody cares! Nobody sees!

MATTHEW. Some folks is gon' see what they see, regardless of what they see.

RUFFRINO. Still –

MATTHEW. Black lives matter? Huh. You a hypocrite, you know that right?

RUFFRINO. What are you talkin' about?

MATTHEW. You talk the talk, but you ain't walkin' the walk. You s'posed to be Mr. Pro Black, Ruffrino X and such, but you don't show a lickuh respect for the "black lives" thass livin' right up under the same roof as you.

RUFFRINO. ...

MATTHEW. Ain't got nothin' to say that, huh?

RUFFRINO. You know what? You right.

MATTHEW. I'm right? Huh. Well, knock me over with a feather!

RUFFRINO. Don't act so surprised. I hear the truth when it's put to me. You right. The revolution starts at home. We ain't never gonna be able to rise up against the oppressive regime of the white man if we fighting in our own homes. That's exactly what they want us to do.

MATTHEW. It sounds like you sayin' you owe me an apology.

RUFFRINO. ...

I'll call you "Pops." Occasionally. That's the best I can do.

> (**MATTHEW** *beams.*)

MATTHEW. You owe yo' mama an apology at least.

RUFFRINO. I didn't mean what I said, she just make me so mad.

MATTHEW. Her and everybody else these days. You just angry in general.

RUFFRINO. I am.

MATTHEW. Well whatchu got to be so angry about?

RUFFRINO. Everything!

MATTHEW. Everything like what?

RUFFRINO. Everything!

MATTHEW. Well, name me jus' one thing. For an example. A for-instance...

RUFFRINO. For instance, right now, I'm pissed off at you!

MATTHEW. Good. And now, why you mad at me for?

RUFFRINO. I'm mad I gotta explain it! I'm mad you don't just get it!

I'm mad you ain't pissed off too!

MATTHEW. What I got to be mad about?

RUFFRINO. EVERYTHING!

MATTHEW. You talk in circles.

...

Teenage angst. That's all that is. You'll grow out of it.

RUFFRINO. (Unless I get shot and killed first.)

(**RUFFRINO** *returns to staring at the TV.*)

MATTHEW. Don't get too comfortable in front of that television, my stories come on in an hour and I gotta see if Juliana comes out of her coma... What's that you watchin' anyhow?

RUFFRINO. MSNBC.

MATTHEW. Is that lady that look like a man on nere? I like it when that lady that look like a man be on nere –

RUFFRINO. Shhhhhhh!

MATTHEW. Shush me again here –

RUFFRINO. This is live coverage. They waiting to hear the results of the grand jury. They decidin' whether or not that racist pig bastard that murdered D'wayne Chambers is gonna be brought up on charges.

MATTHEW. Now where was this? Up in Cleveland?

RUFFRINO. No. That was last week. No charges.

MATTHEW. Oh. This down in Texas?

RUFFRINO. No that was the week before last. No charges.

MATTHEW. This the one in Baltimore den?

RUFFRINO. Nope. That was last month. No charges.

MATTHEW. New York?

RUFFRINO. No charges.

MATTHEW. St. Louis?

RUFFRINO. No charges.

MATTHEW. Minnesota.

RUFFRINO. No. Charges.

MATTHEW. ...

RUFFRINO. This happened in Charlottesville.

MATTHEW. Charlottesville? That's just up the highway a spell –

RUFFRINO. Right.

MATTHEW. It's getting closer then.

RUFFRINO. Right.

> (MATTHEW *and* RUFFRINO *stare at the television.)*

MATTHEW. So they just shot this boy?

RUFFRINO. In the street like a dog. Actually dogs get more respect.

MATTHEW. What was he doing?

RUFFRINO. What do you mean?

MATTHEW. To get himself shot. He must'a been doing something.

RUFFRINO. It doesn't matter what he was doing, he doesn't deserve to be shot and killed like that.

MATTHEW. But he was doin' something? Right?

RUFFRINO. He resisted arrest – allegedly –

MATTHEW. See. There.

RUFFRINO. "See. There." What? That doesn't mean he should be killed. If he was white they wouldn't've –

MATTHEW. But see he's not white. That's the problem with negroes these days. They want rules that don't apply to them, to apply to them.

RUFFRINO. But there should be one set of rules for everybody.

MATTHEW. But that ain't the case. And I ain't sayin' it's fair. But it ain't about bein' fair or unfair, it's about the way things are being the way things are. You gotta accept your circumstances.

See now I wish I could eat collard greens and hog maws, but the doctor said sauteed kale and turkey bacon is better for me. So what I eat? Kale and turkey bacon with a lil EVOO. And that ain't fair, 'cause turkey bacon is lie. But I do it, 'cause them's my rules and if I wanna keep livin' I'ma follow 'em. The problem is negroes these days don't know the rules.

RUFFRINO. We ain't talking about turkey bacon. We talkin' about life. We talkin' about being treated as equals. We're talkin' about not being shot down in the streets and the pigs gettin' off scott-free. There should be –

(**MATTHEW** *lies down on the floor.*)

MATTHEW. There's that word again. "Should." I ain't concerned with "should." I'm concerned with "is." Things "is" the way they "is." And maybe things could change, but they haven't in my lifetime, which leads me to believe that they ain't gonna. Now grab my ankles. It's time for my calisthenics.

(**RUFFRINO** *holds* **MATTHEW**'s *ankles in the sit-up position.*)

MATTHEW. You know what your real problem is, Ruff. You too serious. You like your father.

RUFFRINO. If I had a nickel.

MATTHEW. Your father was a good man – is a good man. He ain't dead.

RUFFRINO. Fifty years to life good?

MATTHEW. Okay. He was a man. Maybe a little less emphasis on the good part. He took care of you and your mother. Until he didn't.

RUFFRINO. Just another black man who fell victim to the systematic separation of the black family perpetuated by the white man since slavery. The black family must be vigilant –

MATTHEW. I don't know about all that...

   (He does sit-ups.)

But one day you'll become a man. Wit' full rights and privileges. You'll encounter many another man on the road. When you do. You stand up straight. Look him square in the eyes. And shake his hand. Firm grip. And you can count yourself. Just as good as any other man. But one day. You'll come across anotha fella. And he gonna be your better. In every conceivable way. And you won't have to bow down formally. It's more carnal than that. His man scent'll top your man scent. And you'll realize. The only reason. You've been in charge. Up to that point. Is because he hadn't been around.

RUFFRINO. You sound like a slave.

MATTHEW. That man for me. Was your father. It's a peculiar thing to have the man that comes for your daughter to be your better. But then I left the do' wide open for folks to be better than me...

RUFFRINO. What are you even talkin' about?

MATTHEW. An old man oughta be able to sit and run off at the mouf and have somebody lissen at him – No. Not just lissen at him, but really pay attention. Pay close attention to him; and his words. 'Cause if you lissen and pay close enough attention, he might just let slip where he been hiding his treasures.

RUFFRINO. Treasures? What are you some kinda pirate or something?

MATTHEW. Wouldn't you like to know.

RUFFRINO. ...

MATTHEW. ...

RUFFRINO. You ain't holding out on us? Is you? Pops?

MATTHEW. Pops? Huh. I like that –

RUFFRINO. Is you?

MATTHEW. So now, all of sudden, you tryin' to hear what I got to say. Now that the subject of money come up.

RUFFRINO. Money? Who said anything about money? Are you hiding money?

MATTHEW. Maybe I is. Maybe I ain't.

RUFFRINO. OH MY GOD! That's why you don't ever have any money. That's why we don't ever see your check –

MATTHEW. Never you mind what I do with my check.

RUFFRINO. Are you kidding me! You got Nadine cleanin' toilets to keep the lights on, all the while you sittin' on stacks.

MATTHEW. Forget it. I shouldn't've brought it up.

RUFFRINO. It take an old negro like you to sit around and hoard dollars. It's not your fault, it's a systematic distrust in financial institutions bred into us to keep us disenfranchised. But still... Where is it? How much you got stashed away –

MATTHEW. Ain't no secret stash. I was just talkin' out the side of neck. Just provin' a point.

RUFFRINO. Which is?

MATTHEW. That you oughta listen to an old man when he talkin'. 'Cause an old man is like a box of chocolate: You never know what you gonna get.

RUFFRINO. I'm tellin' Nadine.

MATTHEW. Don't say nothing to Nadine! Ain't no money. Ain't no stash. Ain't no treasure. So just keep your mouth shut!

RUFFRINO. Let me find out...

Nadine Studies

(Another room in another home. Or at least the suggestion of one.)

*(**NADINE** sits at a table with several books.)*

NADINE. ...

*(**NADINE** studies.)*

...

*(**NADINE** studies.)*

...

*(**NADINE** studies.)*

*(Suddenly, **OFFICER** enters. He's dressed in full police uniform. The chatter from his radio can be heard intermittently. He watches **NADINE**.)*

*(At length, **NADINE** notices him. She panics! She stands and throws her hands up in the air.)*

My hands are up! Don't shoot!

OFFICER. What are –

NADINE. Lovely Maids! I work here. They pay for three hours but they keep the house so clean it only takes me fifteen minutes. Then I do my homework. I know it's wrong. It's stealing.

Technically. But I ain't think it was no reason to call the police on me. Oh lord –

OFFICER. Calm down –

NADINE. Calm down he says. I can't calm down. I can't be arrested. I ain't got the time to be arrested – I ain't got the money to get arrested –

OFFICER. Relax. I'm not the police.

NADINE. You sure look like one.

OFFICER. I mean. I am. A cop. But I'm not here for you. This is my house.

NADINE. Oh. I don't mean to gyp you. It's just it's my only time to study. When I'm not at school, I'm at work, and when I'm not at either one of them, I'm at home. And I can't do my homework at home. I shoulda told somebody y'all was overpaying, but I thought they might give me another house and then I'd lose this time. And I'd flunk out of college. Again. And I also sorta liked the idea of getting paid to do my homework – but that's got nothing to do with you. What do you care about my woes? I'll just be going now and I'll have Lovely Maids adjust the schedule. I'm so sorry. Again.

(She packs her things.)

OFFICER. Don't leave on my account.

NADINE. ...

OFFICER. Why don't you just sit back down, and finish your homework.

NADINE. Now what now?

OFFICER. I mean you been doing it all this time and it hasn't bothered me. So why should it start bothering me now? 'Cause I know?

NADINE. Thass a good point.

OFFICER. Besides, I wouldn't want to be the reason you flunked out of college. Again. So. Please. Stay.

NADINE. I do have a lot of reading to do... Are you sure you don't mind?

OFFICER. As long as you don't mind if I make myself a sandwich.

NADINE. Just don't make a mess, I just finished wiping –
This is your house. By all means.

OFFICER. Thanks.

> (**NADINE** *sits back down at the table. Tentatively.*)

> (**OFFICER** *makes a sandwich.*)

> (**NADINE** *studies.*)

NADINE. ...

> (**OFFICER** *makes a sandwich.*)

OFFICER. ...

> (**NADINE** *studies.*)

NADINE. ...

> (**OFFICER** *makes a sandwich.*)

> (*Suddenly:*)

NADINE.	OFFICER.
This is weird.	What're you studying?
What?	What?
Oh. Biology.	What's weird?
What?	What?

NADINE. This is strange. I'm just gonna go.

> (*She packs her things again.*)

OFFICER. Really. Stay. I'm paying, remember? And...

> (*He shakes crumbs onto the counter.*)

You missed a spot.

NADINE. ...

OFFICER. Seriously. I don't mind the company.

NADINE. Okay…

    (She sits back down. She picks up a book.)

OFFICER. Biology, huh?

NADINE. 101. I'm studying nursing at Lynchburg College. I want to be a neonatal nurse.

OFFICER. Premature babies right?

NADINE. Yeah. I heard somewhere that premies don't cry. Something about that appeals to me.

OFFICER. Hmm.

NADINE. That's the first time I've said that out loud.

OFFICER. Said what out loud?

NADINE. That I want to be a neonatal nurse. That I want to be anything really.

OFFICER. How come?

NADINE. I don't know. Saying it out loud makes it real. And that makes me…nervous.

OFFICER. I bet you'll make a great nurse.

NADINE. You don't know anything about me.

OFFICER. Sure I do. You're clean. Dirt isn't good for babies. And you're good at multitasking. And you're honest… when you get caught at least!

NADINE. I knew it! You just stallin' 'til the boys in blue get here.

OFFICER. I'm kidding.

NADINE. So was I.

OFFICER. …

NADINE. I really am honest though.

OFFICER. Okay. Then what made you tell me you wanted to be a nurse, just now? Honestly.

NADINE. I guess it's 'cause I don't know you. If I told the people that knew me, they would laugh in my face.

OFFICER. Why?

NADINE. Because. I ain't particularly suited to be no nurse. I ain't got no bedside manner to speak of. I'm the worst in a stressful situation. And I can't stand the sight of blood, or people in pain, or needles –

OFFICER. So then why take up nursing?

NADINE. This is starting to feel like an interrogation.

OFFICER. This is a conversation. An actual conversation. Don't ruin it.

NADINE. I don't know. Nursing is a time-honored profession. It's notable. It's a job you can be proud of.

OFFICER. But you can admit that you're not suited for it.

NADINE. It'll come. If I stick with it and keep studying and practicing, what I need will come.

(**OFFICER** *laughs, but not at her.*)

What's so funny?

OFFICER. Hope. It's a female trait.

NADINE. ...

OFFICER. Only a woman can honestly believe that a person can change. That was my wife's favorite thing to say to me. "Don't worry. It'll come."

NADINE. And did it?

OFFICER. It never came. And she went.

NADINE. Oh.

(**NADINE** *studies.*)

...

(**OFFICER** *eats.*)

NADINE. What didn't come?

(OFFICER eats.)

Never mind –

(OFFICER eats.)

OFFICER. You know it was my wife's idea for me to become a cop. She told me to go down to the Emerson building on Tuesday at three p.m. She said it didn't have to be that Tuesday, any Tuesday would do. So I let a few weeks pass because...I'm a man.

NADINE. Mmmhmmm.

OFFICER. And then I went on down there. Turns out it was the recruitment office of the Lynchburg PD. My wife had heard that Lynchburg was so hard up for cops that they were taking anybody who showed up and could walk and chew gum at the same time. And seeing that I fit the bill, I walked right in, 'cause there wasn't a line, I signed my name, and was sworn in as the newest inductee of the Lynchburg Police Academy right there on the spot.

NADINE. That easy huh?

OFFICER. Pretty much.

NADINE. Well what I'm foolin' wit' school for? I oughta just be a cop, right?

OFFICER. You could. They take anybody.

NADINE. Well thanks...

OFFICER. I didn't mean it like that. I'm just saying you could easily become a cop and you don't have to go to school for four years.

NADINE. It's fine. I ain't trying to be no cop. My son would kill me.

OFFICER. Look. I don't want you to think that I'm low-grading the LPD. There are some really great men on the force and they risk everything. Every day. But sometimes I wonder if being a cop was in more of a demand these days would some of us had made the cut. Hell, I probably wouldn't have.

NADINE. What makes you say that?

OFFICER. I'm not exactly suited for it.

NADINE. You look like the type.

OFFICER. Yeah but, I'm non-confrontational. A pacifist really. I don't like to raise my voice if I don't have to. Guns give me the willies, and I don't like donuts.

NADINE. So then why become a cop?

OFFICER. Because. It's a...how'd you put it? "A time-honored profession." Cops are symbols of courage and valor, like modern-day knights.

NADINE. And you ain't that?

OFFICER. But I stuck with it, because like you, my wife hoped that I could change. "Don't worry, it'll come." She said. And so I went to the academy every day, and every day I wondered: Is this the day they'll teach me to be brave? To be noble? Is this the day that I'll learn to be a hero? But that day never came. In fact, they weren't even expecting that of me. Being a cop is just mitigating risk so that you make it home at the end of your shift.

NADINE. Story of my life.

OFFICER. My wife used to remind me. Every day. "Come home safe." Every day. Like if she didn't say it, I would forget and get myself killed. Every day. Like it wasn't the one thought I had racing through my head from the moment I punched in.

NADINE. And so how is that? Being a thing you know you not suited for?

OFFICER. It's exhausting.

NADINE. Oh.

OFFICER. You want my advice?

NADINE. Sure.

OFFICER. Pick another career, quick, before you're seven years in and stuck.

NADINE. Matthew – my dad, was so proud of me the first time I was in college. I know it broke his heart when I flunked out after one semester.

OFFICER. Partied too hard?

NADINE. Pregnant.

OFFICER. Same thing I guess.

NADINE. Don't get me wrong. I love my son. He's the best thing I've done so far.

OFFICER. Of course.

NADINE. I just want my daddy to be proud of me again. So, I'm sticking with it this time. I'm doing it for him.

OFFICER. And I did it for my wife. I'm telling you, it's not enough.

NADINE. Maybe not for you but –

OFFICER. If you could be anything in the world, no limitations or expectations, what would you wanna be when you grew up?

NADINE. You wanna know the awful secret? I like being a cleaning lady. It bothers other people more than it bothers me.

OFFICER. Really?

NADINE. Yeah. I mean a clean toilet is a beautiful thing. It's quantifiable. It's a task with a definitive ending. And once it's done you can look at it and say that it's complete. An achievement. And it makes me feel good about myself. And even though they don't give degrees out for it, it's still got to be worth something.

OFFICER. Sure but –

NADINE. But what?

OFFICER. You mean to tell me that if you could be anything, anything in the entire world, you would choose to clean toilets?

NADINE. Sure?

OFFICER. ...

NADINE. I've never said that out loud either. That's pathetic ain't it?

OFFICER. Yeah. It is. But it's okay. I'm pathetic too.

(**NADINE** *considers this. She realizes she's been insulted.*)

NADINE. I ain't pathetic! And now, you can go on and be pathetic if you want to, but just leave me the hell out of it!

OFFICER. I just –

NADINE. Just because you never cut it as a cop doesn't mean I can't become a nurse. Nursing and policing is two different things. We are two different people. Entirely! And I ain't ask for your advice, or your opinion –

OFFICER. Actually you asked for both.

(**NADINE** *packs her things.*)

NADINE. Well that was my bad. And staying here was a mistake. I won't study here no more, the feng shui is all fucked up anyhow!

(**NADINE** *storms out.*)

(**NADINE** *storms back in.*)

I'm gonna be a nurse, damn it! I'm gonna be a neonatal fuckin' nurse, and I'm gonna nurse the hell out of little babies that don't cry. And I'm gonna be damn good at it too. I'll become the person I need to be, and I ain't gonna wind up sad and alone and pathetic like you! And you can put that in the bank!

(**NADINE** *storms out again.*)

OFFICER. ...

(**OFFICER** *considers all.*)

Diaspora

(A post-apocalyptic wasteland, or at least the suggestion of one.)

(RUFFRINO is garbed in post-apocalyptic armor; a pastiche of everyday found objects. He wields a righteous, futuristic rifle.)

(CAGEDBIRD99, of a similar age, is dressed similarly, save for a lucha mask that obscures her face. She's outfitted with a bazooka.)

(They fend off the zaliens [zombie aliens].)

CAGEDBIRD99. Cover me!

RUFFRINO. I got your back, Cagedbird.

(He zaps a zalien.)

CAGEDBIRD99. Thanks, RuffandRino. I can always count on you!

(They fend off the zaliens.)

RUFFRINO. Zalien scout three o'clock. Decapitate him before he has a chance to alert the zalien infantry –

CAGEDBIRD99. Too late! Check your radar. There's a level-seven zalien army headed our way. They've got a tank! Retreat! Retreat! –

RUFFRINO. No! Let's stand our ground. I'm trying to unlock the Tantalite Broadsword. I need the XP.

CAGEDBIRD99. In that case…IT'S. ABOUT. TO GO. DOWN.

(They brace for the onslaught of zalien soldiers –)

(Suddenly: the whisper of a sniper's bullet.)

(RUFFRINO collapses to the ground silently.)

[Projection: RUFFandRINO has been sniped by REDNECK_SWAG.]

(A second bullet.)

*(**CAGEDBIRD99** is also hit. She slumps over.)*

[Projection: CAGEDBIRD99 has been owned by REDNECK_SWAG.]

(They lie on the ground. Dead.)

CAGEDBIRD99. ...

RUFFRINO. ...

*(**RUFFRINO** respawns.)*

Fuck you redneck_swag!

*(**REDNECK_SWAG**, a disembodied teenage boy's voice:)*

REDNECK_SWAG. *(Voice-over.)* Fuck you. I'm the master! Bow down to your master! BOW DOWN!

*(**CAGEDBIRD99** respawns.)*

CAGEDBIRD99. Sniping is for noobs. It's cheap.

REDNECK_SWAG. *(Voice-over.)* WANH! WANH! WANH! FUCKYOU!

RUFFRINO. NO, FUCKYOU –

CAGEDBIRD99. Ignore him. He's just trolling us.

RUFFRINO. I bet your mom and dad are cousins, you inbred fuck –

REDNECK_SWAG. *(Voice-over.)* FUCK YOU. NIGGER!! YOU FUCKING NIGGERS. EAT SHIT AND DIE. NIGGERS!! NIGGER! FUCKING NIGGER!

RUFFRINO. You white trash piece of shit –

REDNECK_SWAG. *(Voice-over.)* FUCK YOU!! DIE NIGGER. DIEEEE! DIIIIIIIEEEEEE!!! –

> *[Projection: REDNECK_SWAG has logged off.]*

RUFFRINO. FUUUUCCCKKK!!

CAGEDBIRD99. Br'er. My ears.

RUFFRINO. Sorry. That shit really pisses me off – I FUCKIN' HATE WHITE PEOPLE!

CAGEDBIRD99. What are you supposed to do when the rage overwhelms you?

RUFFRINO. Count ten!

CAGEDBIRD99. So...

RUFFRINO. One,two,three,four –

CAGEDBIRD99. Slowly. Breathe.

RUFFRINO. Five...six...seven...eight...nine...ten.

CAGEDBIRD99. Better?

RUFFRINO. Yeah.

CAGEDBIRD99. Within you is a seed of great change, but you can't let anger blind you. Remember: Anger is a stone cast into a wasp's nest.

RUFFRINO. Deep.

> ...

> Thanks.

CAGEDBIRD99. For what?

RUFFRINO. For always being the Martin to my Malcolm.

CAGEDBIRD99. Did you just compare me to Dr. King? Honored, br'er.

RUFFRINO. I mean it. I don't fit in with the zombies at school. I don't fit with the zombies at home. It's like, where do I belong? Ya know?

CAGEDBIRD99. I know exactly how you feel.

RUFFRINO. Of course you do. You not sleep like everybody else. Before I heard you broadcasting your poetry over Xbox Live I thought I was the only conscience black kid in the whole world. I know you supposed to be all kumbaya and shit, but there's rage in your poetry. It spoke to me. We're like soulmates.

(Awkward.)

CAGEDBIRD99. Speaking of which...I've been working on a new piece.

RUFFRINO. Lay it on me.

CAGEDBIRD99. It's called "Language of the Outnumbered."

RUFFRINO. I like it already.

CAGEDBIRD99. It's fresh so, bear with me.

(Slam poetry.)

We meet over time and space

Yet our words are the same

Despite our difference, we're the same

Because I'm broken and you broke

We use the same words to break

We use the same words to cry

The same words to hurt

We speak the same language, you and I

The language of the outnumbered

(Suddenly, **MATTHEW** *enters in his bathrobe.)*

MATTHEW. What the – What is this?

RUFFRINO. I'm playing Diaspora.

CAGEDBIRD99. Who's that?

RUFFRINO. Matthew. The old man that lives in our house.

CAGEDBIRD99. Oh. I got one of those too.

MATTHEW. Well pause this mess. My stories is on and I told you not to let me nap too long.

RUFFRINO. I can't pause it. It's live.

MATTHEW. What's live?

RUFFRINO. Diaspora. I'm online.

MATTHEW. Well I'ma online yo' butt if you don't turn this mess off. I'm missin' my stories.

RUFFRINO. Yo, Cagedbird –

CAGEDBIRD99. I get it. You gotta go. My thumbs hurt anyway. I need food. Later, br'er.

RUFFRINO. Later days.

> (**RUFFRINO** *and* **MATTHEW** *exit.*)
>
> [*Projection: RUFFandRINO has logged off.*]
>
> (**CAGEDBIRD99** *is alone in the space. She removes her mask to reveal that she's a teenage white girl.*)
>
> (*She takes up a hidden pair of forearm crutches, revealing that she is physically disabled.*)
>
> (*She exits.*)
>
> [*Projection: CAGEDBIRD99 has logged off.*]

The Witherspoon Family Curse

(The kitchen/cotton field.)

(MATTHEW and RUFFRINO in the kitchen.)

(They sit in front of the TV. MATTHEW wields the video game controller.*)

RUFFRINO. Don't just stand there. Shoot!

MATTHEW. Somebody's a-comin'.

RUFFRINO. I know. Shoot him!

MATTHEW. Why I wanna go an' do that for?

RUFFRINO. Pops! That's a zalien footsoldier. Half-zombie, half-alien, hell-bent on the destruction of mankind!

MATTHEW. Well, heck, I betta shoot him then.

RUFFRINO. He's biting you!

MATTHEW. Well how do I shoot?

RUFFRINO. Press the A button.

MATTHEW. Now which one is that now?

RUFFRINO. Green! Green! Green!

MATTHEW. Oh. I can't see – hand me my glasses.

RUFFRINO. It's too late! The zalien swarm has overrun your position. They're eating your brains.

MATTHEW. Oh my. That is gruesome. That is...what is that?

RUFFRINO. It's his spleeeen!

MATTHEW. And this don't turn your stomach none?

---

*A license to produce *Br'er Cotton* does not include performance usage rights for any third-party or copyrighted video games. Licensees should create their own sound effects or use sound effects in the public domain.

RUFFRINO. This is nothing. When the zalien queen bites you, your stomach explodes and your last meal splatters on the screen. Nachos!

(**MATTHEW** *stares at* **RUFFRINO**. *He smiles.*)

Why are you making that dopey face?

MATTHEW. Nothin'. You just acting like your old self just now. Before you got so deep off in them books your daddy sent you.

RUFFRINO. Before I woke up you mean?

MATTHEW. If that's whachu wanna call it – before you started mouthin' off, and gettin' into trouble at school – Now, explain to me again, what was you plannin' to do today?

RUFFRINO. I was gonna wake them up.

MATTHEW. Who?

RUFFRINO. The zombies.

MATTHEW. With lighter fluid and a hatchet.

RUFFRINO. Yes.

MATTHEW. You was gonna wake them up?

RUFFRINO. Yes.

MATTHEW. 'Cause they asleep?

RUFFRINO. Comatose.

MATTHEW. Okay, so let's say...best-case scenario you wake them up. Then what?

RUFFRINO. Then they'll see.

MATTHEW. See what exactly?

RUFFRINO. The truth.

MATTHEW. 'Cause they awake? They got they eyes open? They can see the truth?

RUFFRINO. Right.

MATTHEW. Okay. Then what?

RUFFRINO. Then what, what?

MATTHEW. Then what happens, all the people is woke and they eyes is open. And they walkin' round seein' the truth and thangs. Then what happen?

RUFFRINO. Then we change things.

MATTHEW. Change? Is that what you after? You trying to change things?

RUFFRINO. Yes. I'm trying to change the world –

> (**MATTHEW** *laughs.*)
>
> (*And laughs.*)
>
> (*And laughs.*)
>
> (*And cries and laughs.*)

I guess I missed the joke.

MATTHEW. This being my last day on Earth, thas probably gon' be my last good laugh. I thank you for it.

RUFFRINO. What's so funny?

MATTHEW. You. You doin' all this for change! That's rich.

RUFFRINO. ...

MATTHEW. Boy, don't you know you ain't capable of changing nothing but your underwear. You gon' change the world? Huh.

RUFFRINO. Why not me? I gotta chance. I got more of a chance than you. Because I'm doing something. I'm trying. You don't do nothing.

MATTHEW. I beg your pardon. Doing nothin' is an art and I've mastered it. Second off, I ain't got no aims at changin' the world. 'Cause I know what I am.

RUFFRINO. Asleep.

MATTHEW. No. I'm a Witherspoon. Of the Amherst County Witherspoons.

RUFFRINO. Meaning?

MATTHEW. Meaning, the Witherspoons ain't no revolutionary figures. We ain't the changers. We the carry-own-ers. We the gettin'-by-ers.

RUFFRINO. You a crazy old fool. You know that Matthew?

MATTHEW. Witherspoons ain't remarkable. We don't do no revolutionizing. If and when it's time for that, we leave that work to better men than us. We become the minions. The pawns. We wind up casualties. The ones that make up the big numbers. They may etch our tiny Witherspoon name on giant monuments. One tiny name out of millions of other tiny names, but they ain't building no statues of no Witherspoons. 'Cause we the stay-out-of-it-ers. You come from a long line of that-ain't-got-nothing-to-do-with-me-ers.

RUFFRINO. So you mean to tell me, that no other Witherspoon? Ever? Anywhere? Did anything revolutionary? None of us have done anything of any importance? Ever?

MATTHEW. That is correct.

RUFFRINO. …

MATTHEW. The last Witherspoon who tried was your great-great-great-great-great-granduncle Ingraham Witherspoon. Back in 1865 –

RUFFRINO. 1865!

MATTHEW. Your Granduncle Ingraham was a slave. He lived on a cotton plantation. Right here in Amherst County. It was just down twenty-nine a ways, back behind where the old Food Lion used to be. It's towards the end of the war. Confederates was losin'. Losin' bad.

They desperate. They decree that slaves could enlist. "General Order Numba Fourteen." Say it's for a new black infantry startin' up down in Richmond. Say if they fight for honor and country – two things that ain't never served no Witherspoon, mind you... If they fight true they can earn they freedom. They'll be paid a wage. And given a brand-new uniform with a pair of fine leather boots. Now, your Granduncle Ingraham wasn't no fool. Every generation or so we get us a brilliant one. He was a brilliant one. I think you might be one too. I thought your mother was one but she... Anyhow. He was like you. Could see things for what they were and was pissed off about it. He knew better than to believe them white folk, 'specially when they was desperate. But he had a plan. He was gon' "change" things.

So he signed on the dotted line, with an "X," 'cause he couldn't write. And he went off with that man to Richmond. And now while they was trainin' and drillin' during the day, nights he was creepin' round in the shadows, whispering in negroes' ears. Sayin' things like, "Why should we fight for honor and country? We oughta fight for ourselves." And before long he had him a coup in the works.

RUFFRINO. Dope. So then what happened?

MATTHEW. He died by firing squad.

RUFFRINO. What – How?

MATTHEW. The Witherspoon family curse is how. Whispered the right thing to the wrong person. Some other pawn ratted him out. But them Confederates kept they word. They set him free. So to speak. And they sent his uniform to his momma.

RUFFRINO. Is this another one of your old man treasure tales.

MATTHEW. It's true. I got his uniform to prove it.

RUFFRINO. You have Granduncle Ingraham's uniform. You have a Confederate uniform. From 1865?

MATTHEW. Everything 'cept the boots.

RUFFRINO. Where? I've never seen it.

MATTHEW. I ain't never showed it to you.

RUFFRINO. Where is it then?

MATTHEW. It's safe. Bought one of them Space Bags. Sucked it flat with your momma's vacuum. They waterproof ya know?

RUFFRINO. The uniform?

MATTHEW. The Space Bags!

RUFFRINO. And you've got it stashed somewhere in this house?

MATTHEW. It's around.

RUFFRINO. ...

MATTHEW. ...

RUFFRINO. What else you got hid around here?

MATTHEW. Wouldn't you like to know.

RUFFRINO. ...

MATTHEW. ...

RUFFRINO. Where's the money, Matthew?

MATTHEW. Oh, it's in the – Ha. Ha. You ain't slick. There ain't no money!

> (**MATTHEW** *exits.*)
>
> (**RUFFRINO** *considers all.*)
>
> (*The kitchen sinks a few more inches.*)
>
> (**RUFFRINO** *discovers a bowl peeking through the linoleum.*)

I Feel Like My Time Ain't Long

(The cotton field.)

(Large, bright harvest moon overhead.)

*(**GRANDFATHER** wears a cotton sack. He gives another to **SON**.)*

*(**MOTHER** stands nearby with a cotton sack.)*

GRANDFATHER. Don't just stand there like time on a monument. Get to work.

SON. I don't know how.

GRANDFATHER. It's easy enough. It's in your blood.

(He demonstrates.)

This here the stalk. This here the boll. When this boll get good and ready, and not a second before, it'll open up and there: King Cotton.

(He pulls off a lock of cotton.)

*(**SON** follows his example.)*

Be careful now –

SON. Ouch!

GRANDFATHER. That's the burr. They prick a little at first. But you'll have a callus 'fore long.

SON. How much cotton you think I can pick, Grandfather?

GRANDFATHER. Well, I picked five hundred pounds in a day once, Son. But that's when I was a young man. I was 'bout your age, but I was built.

MOTHER. And ask him how much he made for the five hundred pounds of cotton he picked.

SON. How much did you make, Grandfather?

MOTHER.	GRANDFATHER.
Ten dollars.	Ten dollars.

SON. Mother, you've heard this story before?

MOTHER. Surprised you made it this long without hearing it, Son.

GRANDFATHER. Five hundred pure pounds of white gold in one twenty-four-hour time span. And there wasn't a burr or leaf or a twig in the lot. Some fellas used to take and put stones in they bag to make it weigh out more. But I took pride in my work. No gettin' over for me – Now, pay attention to what you doin'. You leavin' cotton in that burr. That's leaving money on the vine.

SON. How you get it to come out so clean?

GRANDFATHER.	MOTHER.
Practice.	Practice.

SON. Wouldn't it be easier to just take the whole thing off? I hear they have machines that can separate them now.

GRANDFATHER. That's the problem with folks nowadays. Think everything oughta be controlled by a button. You gon' learn to do it like I say or you'll be up all night cow-lickin'.

SON. Cow-lickin'? What's that?

MOTHER. That's when you spread out the burrs and the seeds in front of a fire. Easier to get the stray fibers out when they hot.

SON. I'd rather do that, than to be out here all night.

GRANDFATHER. Nonsense. Cotton pickin' by the harvest moon? Moonlight just as bright as the sun. Remind me of them cotton pickin' days when I was a youngster. Folks used to say they was just as good as the cotton pickin' days before the war. It was a big to-do. Everybody helpin' everybody else. We all had cotton to pick so we made a party out of it. Negroes can make a party out of anything. We pick one field, fast, 'cause we was all workin' together. And we a move on to the next. And we didn't quit workin' 'til every field was picked clean. But there was lots of food to be ate and liquor to be drunk. Used to be a prize for the person who picked the most. I won with them five hundred pounds. Beat out that pretty boy, Willie Lavender, who up to that point held the record for most cotton picked in a day. And he was almos' twice my size.

SON. What did you win, Grandfather?

GRANDFATHER. A jug of moonshine. My daddy 'llowed me to drank it too. He say if I work as good as a man, I oughta be able to drink as good as one. I was proud. Still am. I out-picked grown men.

And that night I got drunk like a man. And I danced. And I sang them songs we always sang.

SON. So let's make a deal. If I pick more than you, I can have a swig of that whiskey you keep under the bathroom sink.

MOTHER. No deal.

SON. Mother –

GRANDFATHER. Pick five hundred pounds and then we'll talk.

(GRANDFATHER, MOTHER, and SON pick cotton by the harvest moon.)

(GRANDFATHER begins to hum. His humming soon becomes a song. As he sings, their picking keeps time with the music.*)

---

*A license to produce Br'er Cotton does not include a performance license for any third-party or copyrighted music. Licensees should create an original composition or use music for "I Feel Like My Time Ain't Long" that is in the public domain. For further information, please see the Music and Third-Party Materials Use Note on page iii.

I FEEL LIKE, I FEEL LIKE, LORD,
I FEEL LIKE MY TIME AIN'T LONG;
I FEEL LIKE, I FEEL LIKE, LORD,
I FEEL LIKE MY TIME AIN'T LONG.
SAW DEATH IN THE MIRR' THE OTHER DAY.

MOTHER.
I FEEL LIKE MY TIME AIN'T LONG.

GRANDFATHER.
WON'T LEAVE ME 'LONE, WON'T GO AWAY.

MOTHER.
I FEEL LIKE MY TIME AIN'T LONG.

GRANDFATHER & MOTHER.
I FEEL LIKE, I FEEL LIKE, LORD,
I FEEL LIKE MY TIME AIN'T LONG;
I FEEL LIKE, I FEEL LIKE, LORD,
I FEEL LIKE MY TIME AIN'T LONG;

GRANDFATHER.
CAN SEE HEAVEN'S GATE FROM MY FRONT DO'.

> (**GRANDFATHER** *gestures for* **SON** *to fill in the blank.*)

SON.
I FEEL LIKE MY TIME AIN'T LONG?

GRANDFATHER.
JUST LIKE BR'ER COTTON, CAIN'T TAKE IT NO MO'.

MOTHER.
I FEEL LIKE MY TIME AIN'T LONG.

GRANDFATHER.
GONNA PUT ALL MY TOILIN' AND BURDENS DOWN.

GRANDFATHER & MOTHER.
I FEEL LIKE MY TIME AIN'T LONG.

GRANDFATHER.

LISTENIN' FO' DA GLORY TRUMPETS SOUND.

GRANDFATHER & MOTHER.

I FEEL LIKE MY TIME AIN'T LONG.

ALL.

I FEEL LIKE, I FEEL LIKE, LORD,
I FEEL LIKE MY TIME AIN'T LONG;
I FEEL LIKE, I FEEL LIKE, LORD,
I FEEL LIKE MY TIME AIN'T LONG.

(The chorus is repeated as the trio picks cotton by the moonlight.)

Morning

(The kitchen/cotton field.)

(The cotton field has grown farther into the kitchen. Vines and cotton stalks abound.)

(A large oak tree has grown in the middle of the kitchen, overturning the table and chairs.)

(RUFFRINO *and* **NADINE** *enter; they are both dressed in funeral blacks.)*

NADINE. You hungry?

> **(RUFFRINO** *marvels at the tree. He alone can see it.)*

RUFFRINO. Naw.

NADINE. Sister from the church brought over a casserole. I can warm that up?

RUFFRINO. I'm good.

> **(NADINE** *notices the table. She moves it. She moves the chairs. She considers all.)*

NADINE. It was a nice service.

RUFFRINO. Nobody was there.

NADINE. There was folks there.

RUFFRINO. Not enough. Not for as old as he was.

NADINE. It was a nice service.

RUFFRINO. It was a waste of money, that's what it was.

NADINE. What's it to you? That's how come I work every day. To pay for stuff like this.

RUFFRINO. ...

NADINE. Speaking of which...I picked up a extra shift tonight. You gon' be alright here by yourself?

RUFFRINO. You going to work? Today? You leavin' me –

NADINE. I got to.

RUFFRINO. We didn't need such a fancy box. We should have put his ass in a Space Bag and called it a damn day.

NADINE. Hush now! It ain't right to speak ill of the dead.

RUFFRINO. So just 'cause he dead I'm supposed to forget that he was spineless old fool. You know the day he died –

NADINE. And I'm glad I made you stay home that day. Least he wasn't by himself.

RUFFRINO. He shoulda died by himself. He was a weak-ass old coward and I wish I had never found it out.

NADINE. What are you talkin' about?

RUFFRINO. He said Witherspoons ain't remarkable. There's nothing special about us.

NADINE. You gotta understand. Matthew comes from a different time –

RUFFRINO. It's probably true though. I mean he wasn't shit. And you... You so nothin' you can't even afford to take a day off cleaning some white man's toilet to mourn your own not-shit father –

NADINE. RUFFRINO! I know you mad and you grieving. But you need to stop!

RUFFRINO. He really had me believing that I was destined to be a nobody too. Just like y'all. But then I remembered; I'm not really a Witherspoon. I mean if you had done things right I woulda been a Fleming like my father. But of course you fucked that up too –

(**NADINE** *slaps him.*)

...

(**RUFFRINO** *sits down in front of the TV. He turns on the video game console and picks up the controller.**)

NADINE. Ruffrino?

(*He ignores her.*)

Ruffrino I...

RUFFRINO. ...

NADINE. I gotta get ready for work.

(**RUFFRINO** *plays the video game console.*)

Don't sit here and play that damn game all day.

(**RUFFRINO** *plays the video game console.*)

Right.

(**NADINE** *exits.*)

(*The kitchen sinks several inches deeper.*)

(**RUFFRINO** *discovers another cotton plant growing under his seat.*)

---

*A license to produce *Br'er Cotton* does not include performance usage rights for any third-party or copyrighted video games. Licensees should create their own sound effects or use sound effects in the public domain.

Nadine Weeps

> *(Another room in another home. Or at least the suggestion of one.)*

> *(**NADINE** cleans.)*

NADINE. ...

> *(**NADINE** cleans.)*

...

> *(**NADINE** cleans.)*

...

> *(**NADINE** breaks.)*

> *(**NADINE** weeps.)*

> *(**NADINE** weeps.)*

> *(**NADINE** weeps.)*

> *(**OFFICER** enters.)*

> *(**NADINE** hides her weeping.)*

OFFICER. Well, if it isn't Nadine Maurice Witherspoon.

NADINE. You figured out my name.

OFFICER. Name, address, date of birth, social security... You'd be surprised how much information you can get when you flash a badge.

> *(He sees her tears.)*

You're crying. I'm sorry –

NADINE. For what? You ain't done nothin'.

OFFICER. I'm sorry. I see a woman crying, I apologize. It's a reflex.

NADINE. Oh.

OFFICER. But I do owe you an apology actually –

NADINE. No. I owe you one. I was rude.

OFFICER. I was rude first. I shouldn't have called you pathetic. Or told you to give up hope. I was miserable. Still am actually. And I guess I wanted company. My shrink calls it emotional contagion. I'm really sorry –

NADINE. I buried my father this morning. Plot 482. Fort Hills Memorial Park.

OFFICER. Are you serious?

NADINE. Yeah. How's that for emotional contagion?

OFFICER. What are you doing here? You should be at home with your family.

NADINE. I can't afford to grieve.

OFFICER. I am so sorry –

NADINE. Stop sayin' you sorry to me.

OFFICER. I'm sorry – Sorry! Sorry –

NADINE. I thought I wanted to be a nurse for him. To make him proud. But I can see now, I was doing it out of spite. I can tell 'cause I ain't got that pit in my stomach no more. Ya know? It was all this anger and resentment towards him that was driving me, 'cause he had such a low opinion of his daughter. Then he went and died thinking he was right about me.

(Pregnant silence.)

OFFICER. So...since you told me to stop apologizing, I'm sorta at a loss for what to say. But I know I should say something. What do you want me to say?

NADINE. You could ask me how I feel. Don't nobody ever ask me how I feel.

OFFICER. Okay. How do you feel, Nadine?

NADINE. Honestly? In this moment, I feel...relief. I got nobody's expectations or disappointments to live up to no more.

OFFICER. Silver lining I guess? What about your son? I'm sure he's proud of you, for not giving up. For trying again –

NADINE. He don't know. Nobody knows. I figured I wouldn't tell nobody, so if and when I quit they wouldn't think any less of me.

OFFICER. So how is your son taking all this?

NADINE. Like he take everything else: personally.

OFFICER. Could you tell me about him?

(NADINE *smiles.*)

NADINE. He's a mess. He's fourteen. He'll be fifteen in June. Ruffrino is his name. He's brilliant. Maybe a little too brilliant. And he's scared. All the time. Every day. He's the spittin' image of his father he is. And he acts up to mask it, the fear, but a mother sees.

OFFICER. So what does his father do about it?

NADINE. He sends him Black Panther books from jail.

OFFICER. Maybe I could talk to him –

NADINE. That's a terrible idea.

OFFICER. Maybe he should talk to a professional. Both of you really. When my wife left me it really helped to confide in someone –

NADINE. I can't afford to confide.

OFFICER. Maybe your pastor could –

NADINE. Look, you don't have to try and fix my problems. My woes ain't got nothin' to do with you.

OFFICER. I can't help it. When I see a woman in distress I have to try and fix it. It's a reflex.

NADINE. But –

>(**OFFICER** *hugs her.* **NADINE** *lets go. She weeps and weeps and weeps until:*)

>(*She laughs and laughs and cries and laughs –*)

OFFICER. What's so funny?

NADINE. Nothin'. It's just you know so much about me. More than anybody else. I think that make you like... my best friend.

>(*They laugh together.*)

OFFICER. Why don't you take the rest of the day off?

NADINE. I can't –

OFFICER. Listen to your BFF. Go be with your son. You two need each other. Now more than ever.

>(*He scribbles on a piece of paper.*)

This is my number. If you need anything. Anything at all, day or night, I'm just a phone call away.

>(**NADINE** *takes the paper.*)

NADINE. Maybe they did teach you something about being noble after all.

Diaspora II

(A post-apocalyptic wasteland, or at least the suggestion of one.)

(RUFFRINO *and* **CAGEDBIRD99** *wear their armor.)*

CAGEDBIRD99. Look alert! There's a couple of zalien scouts on my radar.

RUFFRINO. ...

*(**RUFFRINO** runs forward, shooting aimlessly.)*

CAGEDBIRD99. RuffandRino look out!

*(An axe slices into **RUFFRINO**'s armor. He drops to the ground.)*

[Projection: RUFFandRINO has been slaughtered.]

(CAGEDBIRD99 *waits.)*

RUFFRINO. ...

CAGEDBIRD99. ...

*(**RUFFRINO** respawns.)*

Br'er. What's up with you today? It's like you're trying to get killed.

RUFFRINO. Shut up and play the game.

CAGEDBIRD99. ...

Is something wrong?

RUFFRINO. No.

CAGEDBIRD99. It sure seems like there's –

RUFFRINO. Let's just play the game. Alright?

CAGEDBIRD99. Fine.

RUFFRINO. Fine.

CAGEDBIRD99. We've cleared this quadrant. Let's move on to quadrant four, the enemies are harder but there's more XP –

> *(Suddenly: the whisper of a sniper's bullet.)*

> (**CAGEDBIRD99** *collapses to the ground silently.)*

RUFFRINO. The fuck?

> *[Projection: CAGEDBIRD99 has been sniped by REDNECK_SWAG.]*

Not this shit again.

> *(He takes cover.)*

Why don't you come out you asshole? You a man or nah?

> *(Several more of the sniper's bullets are heard. They miss.)*

Missed me you fucktard. Quit sniping like a little bitch –

> *(Suddenly we hear the approach of a missile. Followed by a loud explosion.)*

> (**RUFFRINO** *is blown back.)*

> *[Projection: RUFFandRINO has been blown to smithereens by REDNECK_SWAG.]*

> (**REDNECK_SWAG** *cackles with glee.)*

REDNECK_SWAG. *(Voice-over.)* DIE YOU FUCKING RETARD NIGGERS DIE!! FUCK YOU NIGGERS!! FUCK YOU NIGGERS!! BURN! BUUURRRNN! BOW DOWN TO YOUR MASTER! BOW DOWN TO YOUR MASTER YOU FUCKING FAGGOT NIGGERS!

[Projection: REDNECK_SWAG has logged off.]

(**CAGEDBIRD99** *respawns.*)

(**RUFFRINO** *respawns.*)

RUFFRINO. FUUUUCCCKK!!

(**RUFFRINO** *begins firing rounds aimlessly.*)

CAGEDBIRD99. Dude. Be careful. I've got friendly fire turned on.

RUFFRINO. Who gives a fuck about this game?

CAGEDBIRD99. You love this game.

RUFFRINO. I hate this shit! I hate all of it!

CAGEDBIRD99. Well they just announced Diaspora2's coming out –

RUFFRINO. Not the fuckin' game – Life! The world! My fuckin' family! I hate all this shit!

CAGEDBIRD99. That sounds like your rage again. You should count –

RUFFRINO. Fuck counting!

CAGEDBIRD99. Why do you let redneck_swag get to you? He's just some loser kid.

RUFFRINO. It's not just him. It's what he stands for.

CAGEDBIRD99. Which is?

RUFFRINO. The corrosive majority perception that "other" somehow means less than.

CAGEDBIRD99. I understand that. Believe me, I do, but –

RUFFRINO. I can't even play a fucking game without being reminded that I'm just some "nigger." That fuckin' word, man! Why the fuck should he call me that? Why?! And I can't do nothing to protect myself from it, there's no weapon to combat that shit. There's no armor I can put on against it. At any moment I can be a "nigger." At any moment I can be less than just because some white muthafucka says so. No matter where I am, no matter what I do, at any moment I can be just some worthless "nigger." THAT FUCKING WORD!

CAGEDBIRD99. He's just a loser kid sitting in a trailer somewhere drinking a Super Gulp of Mountain Dew. He doesn't matter.

RUFFRINO. But loser kids like him grow and kill black kids like us. And they get away with it. I wish I could just crack his head open and find the thing in his brain that makes him racist and pulverize it. But I can't! I'm starting to see that I can't change nothin'. I can't change anybody.

CAGEDBIRD99. Maya Angelou said: If you can't change something, change your attitude –

RUFFRINO. I HATE WHITE PEOPLE!

CAGEDBIRD99. How is that helpful?

RUFFRINO. What are you talking about?

CAGEDBIRD99. Hating back. You can't fight hate with hate.

RUFFRINO. Why the hell not?

CAGEDBIRD99. An eye for an eye makes the whole world blind. That's Gandhi.

RUFFRINO. How 'bout, you take my eye, I fuckin' decapitate you. That's Ruffrino.

CAGEDBIRD99. I –

RUFFRINO. The verdict came back today on the D'wayne Chambers case up in Charlottesville.

CAGEDBIRD99. I heard. No charges.

RUFFRINO. Can you believe that? You would think at this point, with all the backlash these cases are getting that they would've charged him out of guilt. Or to appease us. To set an example. But they setting the example they want to set. That black people don't matter and they're willing to show us this over and over and over and over and over –

CAGEDBIRD99. I'm sorry –

RUFFRINO. Don't say sorry to me. That's what those privileged crackers say to me at school. "I'm sorry." They feel sorry for me. Like it's my problem. Like it's my issue. Like it doesn't affect them. But then they don't have to fear being shot down by the police. So...I'm done. I've done the peaceful protests and the silent vigils. It's time out for peaceful. They need to feel it.

CAGEDBIRD99. What does that mean? You're scaring me, br'er. I've never heard you talk like this. Is there something else going on?

RUFFRINO. What the fuck ELSE needs to be going on? Other than WHAT THE FUCK IS GOING ON!

CAGEDBIRD99. I just –

RUFFRINO. You know, I thought you got it. I thought you understood me. But I'm starting to think you just as sleep as the rest of the zombies.

CAGEDBIRD99. RuffandRino –

RUFFRINO. Get at me when you wake the hell up! –

> *[Projection: RUFFandRINO has logged off.]*

> (**CAGEDBIRD99** *is left alone in the game.*)

CAGEDBIRD99. *(Slam poetry.)* We meet over distance and difference

Yet they name us just the same

Our word for acceptance is right on the tip our tongues

It's... It's... It's...

Our vocabulary fails us

But we have many words for

lonely As many as the Eskimos for snow.

We're both forsaken, you and I

But we understand each other

and our language of the misunderstood

An Acorn

(The kitchen/cotton field.)

*(**RUFFRINO** sits at the dinner table, rummaging through boxes of old keepsakes and bric-a-brac.)*

(He discovers a picture of Matthew. He stares at it a little too long.)

(A breeze stirs the leaves of the tree.)

RUFFRINO. ...

(A breeze still.)

Matthew?

(In response, an acorn falls from the tree and lands on the table.)

*(**RUFFRINO** marvels at it.)*

(Another acorn falls from the tree. It rains acorns. Another. And then another. Another.)

(And then...a Space Bag.)

*(**RUFFRINO** retrieves the bag. He cuts into it with a knife.)*

(He removes a pair of pants and then a Confederate soldier's hat. He places the hat atop his head for safekeeping.)

(He removes a jacket. In the inside pocket he finds bowls of cotton. He marvels at them.)

(He keeps digging. And then: money. Enough money to change their lives.)

Crazy old fool...

*(Just then, **NADINE** can be heard entering the house.)*

*(**RUFFRINO** hastily shoves the money and the uniform back into the Space Bag and, thinking quickly, stashes it under the kitchen sink.)*

*(As **NADINE** enters, **RUFFRINO** realizes he is still wearing the cap. He ducks under the table and stashes the hat.)*

*(**NADINE** wasn't expecting to see **RUFFRINO**, she's still holding her school books. She doubles back to hide them.)*

(They both miss what the other is hiding.)

*(**NADINE** re-enters.)*

NADINE. Why're you under the table?

RUFFRINO. Why do you keep moving the furniture? Everything we got is trash, don't matter where it is.

NADINE. You know who you sound like don't you?

RUFFRINO. ...

NADINE. You hungry? I picked up some Cheesies.

(She holds up an oily brown paper bag.)

RUFFRINO. How come you home so early?

NADINE. I wanted to be here. With you.

RUFFRINO. All of a sudden.

NADINE. No not all of a sudden – Please Ruffrino. I don't want to fight.

(She surveys the room.)

What is all this mess?

RUFFRINO. Matthew's shit.

(**NADINE** *cuts her eyes.*)

Stuff. Matthew's stuff.

NADINE. He was a hoarder and I ain't even know it. Huh. What are you doing with it?

RUFFRINO. Nothing. Looking I guess.

NADINE. Looking for what? His buried treasure?

RUFFRINO. No.

NADINE. I hate to break it to you, but you ain't gon' find nothin' valuable. Unless you know somebody interested in old receipts and bits of paper.

RUFFRINO. And obituaries. That's why nobody was at his funeral. All his friend are dead people.

NADINE. It's sad really. A man live sixty some odd years and what he got to show for it? Bills! Bills he still ain't paid. Bills somebody else gon' have to pay.

RUFFRINO. I thought we shouldn't speak ill of the dead.

NADINE. It ain't about speaking ill. It's the truth. Promise me this, Ruffrino. I don't care where you go or what you do with your life, just promise me you won't be the type of man to make a mess and walk away. Promise me that.

RUFFRINO. Can I get one of them Cheesies?

NADINE. Here. You want me to nuke it?

RUFFRINO. No. I like 'em cold.

NADINE. Nasty. You gon' get sick.

RUFFRINO. What? Is that your medical opinion?

(**NADINE** *considers this.*)

NADINE. I don't know what kind of opinion it is.

RUFFRINO. ...

NADINE. Eat.

> (**RUFFRINO** *unwraps and eats a burger.*)

> (**NADINE** *watches him.*)

This is nice. Us. Talking like civilized people. Sharing a meal, no fighting no –

> (**RUFFRINO** *cuts her off by turning on the television.**)

> (*They watch.*)

> (**RUFFRINO** *eats.* **NADINE** *watches him.*)

> (**NADINE** *watches TV.* **RUFFRINO** *watches* **NADINE.**)

What – What are you looking at?

RUFFRINO. I never noticed how old you are. When I'm just thinking about you, in my mind, you're real young and pretty. But just now, in this light, in that chair right here in this kitchen, you look old...and cracked.

NADINE. Gee. Thanks.

> (*Something on TV catches her attention.*)

Hold on now, turn that up... What in the world is going on in this world?

> (*The sounds of protests and rioting emanate from the television.**)

RUFFRINO. That's Charlottesville!

NADINE. Oh my stars. That is Charlottesville. Looks like a third-world country.

---

*A license to produce *Br'er Cotton* does not include a performance license for any third-party or copyrighted recordings. Licensees should create their own.

RUFFRINO.	NADINE.
This is awesome!	This is terrible.

NADINE. Awesome? What could possibly be awesome about this.

RUFFRINO. Finally somebody's doing something. They standing up. They fighting back!

NADINE. By tearing up they own neighborhoods, looting, starting fires in they own streets –

RUFFRINO. What they neighborhoods ever done for them? What the streets ever done for them? I gotta get to Charlottesville!

NADINE. Excuse me?

RUFFRINO. I need to be there. This is my moment. The revolution is being televised. It's my time to wake everybody up!

NADINE. You a fool if you think I'm 'bout to let you go get involved in that mess.

RUFFRINO. You a fool if you think you can stop me.

NADINE. How you gon' get there?

RUFFRINO. I'll take the Greyhound.

NADINE. If you can afford a Greyhound you should be able to put some money on some of these bills we got around here.

RUFFRINO. Is that all you think about? Bills?

NADINE. When you ain't got the money to pay the bills, it tend to be the first thing on your mind.

RUFFRINO. Some things are bigger than bills, Nadine.

NADINE. I wouldn't know. Now you ain't going to no Charlottesville! They causin' enough trouble on they own. What good you gon' do being just another monkey in the crowd?

RUFFRINO. I'm going.

NADINE. You ain't!

RUFFRINO. Try and stop me.

> *(They face off. An impasse.)*
>
> **(RUFFRINO** *attempts to push past* **NADINE.***)*
>
> **(NADINE** *grabs* **RUFFRINO** *by the shirt. She begins to hit him about the head and shoulders. Each word is punctuated by a punch or a slap.)*

NADINE.	RUFFRINO.
You. Ain't. Going. Nowhere.	Get off of me! Let me go!
What's. Wrong. With. You?	Stop!
You. Trying. To. Get. Killed!	Stop!
Huh! You. Wanna. Go. To.	STOP!
Jail?	STOP!

> **(RUFFRINO** *is finally able to break free of* **NADINE.***)*

RUFFRINO. FUUUCKK!! Wake up Nadine! There's scarier things than jail! There's bigger shit than death!

> *(He storms out. Slams the door!)*
>
> *(The kitchen sinks: down, down, and down. Vines and cotton stalks push out of every crack and crevice.)*
>
> *(The cotton field encroaches deeper into the house.)*
>
> **(NADINE** *is exhausted and weeping.)*
>
> **(RUFFRINO** *exits.)*
>
> **(NADINE** *doesn't object.)*

Nadine Waits

(**NADINE** *sits waiting.*)

(*As she waits, the cotton field overtakes the house. It overgrows her. Vines and stalks of cotton root her to the chair.*)

(*Yet* **NADINE** *waits.*)

(*Moonlight gives way to sunrise, then morning.*)

(**NADINE** *picks up the phone. She dials the number from the piece of paper.*)

NADINE. Hey, um... Officer... I just realized I don't even know your name. Which makes this crazy. This is crazy. It's so early. I don't know why I'm calling... Well I do. But I don't think that I should be. You're kind of a stranger. But I'm worried about Ruffrino, my son. We had a big fight, and he been gone all night. I think he might be in some kinda trouble. I just got this feelin' of impending disaster. Like it's lurking round in the furrows. And more so than usual. And it feels like I been here before. I know I have actually. And just like then, I can't move. Stuck in this rut. 'Cause the past ain't no great comfort. And the future don't seem to be offerin' no solace. I'm not calling because I want you to do anything. It's my problem. Really. I just wanted someone to listen. I guess your voicemail will have to do for the moment –

(**RUFFRINO** *returns.*)

(**NADINE** *hangs up the phone.*)

You back.

RUFFRINO. I need to prepare.

NADINE. Prepare for what?

RUFFRINO. War.

NADINE. I hate to break it to you, but you ain't going to no war –

RUFFRINO. I'm going to Charlottesville, Nadine and you can't stop me –

NADINE. I know about the money.

RUFFRINO. You found –

NADINE. The eighty-three dollars and eleven cents you had hid under your bed.

RUFFRINO. Oh. That money.

NADINE. I spent it.

RUFFRINO. You what?

NADINE. At least I'm going to. I'm going right down to Appalachian Power and putting that money on the light bill. So there, you ain't got no money for no Greyhound no more.

RUFFRINO. Then I'll walk if I have to.

NADINE. Ruffrino –

RUFFRINO. You so damn sleep! You really think money is gonna stop me from doing what I need to do? I ain't you.

NADINE. I been sittin' here all night. Thinking. 'Bout you. 'Bout my life. 'Bout this family. I feel like I turned gray overnight. We hangin' on by a thread. Danglin'. And the only thing that can save us, the only thing that can get us on solid ground again is you. I need you to save us, Ruffrino –

RUFFRINO. That's what I'm trying to do! I'm trying to save the world, Nadine! For us! Don't you understand that?

*(**NADINE** uproots herself from the chair.)*

(She faces off with **RUFFRINO.***)*

*(***RUFFRINO*** braces himself.)*

*(***NADINE*** reaches out...and embraces him.)*

*(***RUFFRINO*** resists.)*

(But she holds on to him.)

NADINE. I don't wanna fight with you no more. I can't.

> *(She holds on to* **RUFFRINO.** *He lets go, he finds comfort in her arms.)*

You becomin' a man. And I can't make your decisions for you.

RUFFRINO. ...

NADINE. You remindin' me of your father right now. He was afraid too once. And he stood right where you standing.

Between one decision and another. And I couldn't do nothin' then either. So I tol' him the same thing I'ma tell you: Make the right choice.

> *(***NADINE*** gives **RUFFRINO** back his bookbag.)*

> *(She begins to exit.)*

RUFFRINO. Where are you going?

NADINE. Where I'm always going. To work.

> *(She exits.)*

> *(***RUFFRINO*** is torn with indecision. He teeters from one notion to the next.)*

> *(He gathers the money and the uniform from under the sink and places all on the table.)*

> *(He considers. He paces.)*

(He turns on the video game console. Picks up the controller.)

(He's transported to the world of Diaspora.)

RUFFRINO. Cagedbird! Cagedbird!

[Projection: CAGEDBIRD99 is offline.]

I'm sorry. I need you. Please! I need your help. You're the only one who understands! I need you...

(He breaks.)

I need you.

[Projection: CAGEDBIRD99 has logged on.]

CAGEDBIRD99. Hey... Sorry. I was on invisible mode, redneck_swag was trolling me again.

RUFFRINO. Guess where I'm headed?

CAGEDBIRD99. To school. What time is it where you are?

RUFFRINO. I don't know. Early. Guess again.

CAGEDBIRD99. I don't know, just tell me.

RUFFRINO. Charlottesville.

CAGEDBIRD99. Virginia?

RUFFRINO. Yes.

CAGEDBIRD99. They're rioting in Charlottesville. Aren't they? It's all over the news. Why would you wanna go there?

RUFFRINO. You just answered your own question.

CAGEDBIRD99. It looks dangerous.

RUFFRINO. The world is dangerous, Cagedbird. And if the white man is gonna continue to use violence against us at some point we should start using it back. If they kill us –

CAGEDBIRD99. Then what? You kill them?

RUFFRINO.   Maybe. Maybe then they'll pay attention.
I'm sick of it being my issue. I'm tired of white people
hurting us. I'm tired of white people killing us and
getting away with it! I FUCKING HATE WHITE
PEOPLE –

CAGEDBIRD99. I'M WHITE!

RUFFRINO. What? What do you mean?

CAGEDBIRD99. I'm...white. And that's a weird thing for
me to say. I don't think I've ever said it before because
it's never mattered before. Because so much of me, my
identity is CP. That's Cerebral Palsy, which is a little like
a stroke that happens when you're born...

RUFFRINO. Cagedbird, what the fuck are you talking about?

CAGEDBIRD99. Since I can remember I've always described
myself in those terms. "Cerebral Palsy, which is a little
like a stroke that happens when you're born." In terms
of my condition. So being white was never an issue.

RUFFRINO. So then why didn't you tell me?

CAGEDBIRD99. Because. I was just happy to find a friend
who didn't see me as broken. Because that's how I see
myself, and that's how you see yourself. And we bonded
over that. Because I know what it's like to be judged by
sight alone. To have to make excuses for being born the
way you were born.

RUFFRINO. So you think being black is the same as being
a retard.

CAGEDBIRD99. That's so ugly. That's not you talking.

RUFFRINO. How do you know? You don't know who I am,
'cause apparently I don't know who the fuck you are.

CAGEDBIRD99. I know you're better than that. I know you
know me. You actually see me. I know I don't understand

your struggle completely... I never could. Or you mine for that matter. But we speak the same language you and I –

RUFFRINO. The fuck we do. I speak the truth and you're a fuckin' liar.

CAGEDBIRD99. I'm sorry –

RUFFRINO. You betrayed me –

CAGEDBIRD99. I'm sorry.

RUFFRINO. Don't say sorry to me!

>   *(***RUFFRINO*** seethes.* **CAGEDBIRD99** *shrinks.)*

CAGEDBIRD99. ...

RUFFRINO. ...

CAGEDBIRD99. Do you hate me now?

RUFFRINO. Yeah...

But not because you're white.

>   *[Projection: RuffandRino has logged off.]*
>
>   (***CAGEDBIRD99*** *is left alone in the game.)*
>
>   *(She breaks.)*

CAGEDBIRD99. *(Slam poetry.)* We meet over pain and loss

Pain of judgment and anger at the loss

The loss of nothing; yet missing something

Frustration because we're not quite sure what

And the words build into a tidal wave

That breaks upon the shore

And it breaks us and erodes us

It strips us, you and I

But we understand each other

And our language of the festering

>*(Simultaneously:)*

>**(RUFFRINO** *takes the items from the Space Bag. He undresses, putting on the Confederate uniform.)*

>*(As he puts on the jacket, he discovers several bullet holes in it.)*

>*(As he places the hat atop his head, the final piece, the kitchen begins to sink gravely. Down and down and down.)*

>*(The kitchen is overwhelmed by the cotton field. The cotton field has take back the house.)*

>*(The leaves on the oak tree begin to stir.)*

>**(RUFFRINO** *removes the axe from his bookbag.)*

>*(He begins to chop down the tree. It's a small axe and a big tree, and as he chops, his anger and rage and frustrations grow like vines.)*

>**(RUFFRINO** *chops.)*

RUFFRINO. …

>**(RUFFRINO** *chops.)*

   …

>**(RUFFRINO** *chops.)*

   …

>*(Suddenly,* **OFFICER** *enters.)*

OFFICER. Hello? Hello? I'm looking for Nadine Witherspoon –

(**RUFFRINO** *freezes. He holds the axe up.*)

Ruffrino?

(**RUFFRINO** *sees red. He attacks* **OFFICER** *with the axe.*)

(*They struggle over the axe.*)

(*They wrestle.*)

(*They wrestle.*)

(*They wrestle.*)

(*They wrestle.*)

(*Until,* **RUFFRINO** *takes* **OFFICER**'s *gun.*)

(*He aims the gun at* **OFFICER**.)

(**OFFICER** *puts his hands up.*)

Listen. Kid. Don't shoot.

RUFFRINO. ...

OFFICER. Look. My hands are up. Don't shoot.

I don't know what's going on here, but...you don't have to do this.

RUFFRINO. ...

OFFICER. I'm a friend. I'm a friend of your mother. She cleans my house –

(**RUFFRINO** *clicks off the safety and concentrates his aim.*)

RUFFRINO. ...

OFFICER. Listen. I'm here because she called me. She said she was worried about you –

RUFFRINO. Shut up!

OFFICER. Ruffrino!

RUFFRINO. Stop saying my name!

OFFICER. I'm a friend of your mom. My name is –

RUFFRINO. I don't want to know your name!

OFFICER. Don't do this. Please, Ruff–

RUFFRINO. Stop saying my fuckin' name!

OFFICER. Look, don't do this to your mom. Okay? She's been through enough.

RUFFRINO. What do you know about it?

OFFICER. We're friends. We talk. Hey, I bet you didn't know she was back in college.

RUFFRINO. That's a lie!

OFFICER. No. She's studying to be a nurse. A baby nurse. She's been taking night school classes – She doesn't need this. You don't need this. Just put the gun down, I'm sure we can get this all figured out.

RUFFRINO. No! NO! It doesn't matter... I see it now. I don't need to go to Charlottesville. The revolution starts right here! Right now! With us. Men like you are shooting kids like me, every day –

OFFICER. I haven't shot anybody!

RUFFRINO. But white men just like you are shooting black kids just like me, every day AND GETTING AWAY WITH IT!

OFFICER. I'm not a villain here, kid. Hell, I'm not even a hero. I'm not the problem –

RUFFRINO. Yeah...but you look like it.

> (**RUFFRINO** *fires the gun.*)
>
> (*The faces of slaughtered black boys flash across his mind.*)

(He fires again.)

(And then again.)

(And again. And again.)

(Blackout.)

Epilogue

(The cotton field.)

*(**MOTHER**, a new mother, cradling an infant. Timeless.)*

*(This is a lullaby. **MOTHER** fills the beats [...] with song.*)*

MOTHER. Everyone was glad to live in such close proximity to heaven, it made them content to have heaven's front door be in rock-skippin' distance. But being so close and yet so far away kept Br'er Cotton tossing and turning at nights.

...

"Why," he thought. "Why can I only enjoy heaven in my dreams?"

...

The unfairness of it all infuriated Br'er Cotton to the point where he grew stones in his stomach. 'Til this one day, no special day in particular, save it was the day that he finally made his decision. On this very ordinary day Br'er Cotton decided he could take it no longer. He was gonna break into heaven.

...

...

---

*A license to produce *Br'er Cotton* does not include a performance license for any third-party or copyrighted music. Licensees should create an original composition or use music in the public domain. For further information, please see the Music and Third-Party Materials Use Note on page iii.